MW01503856

DISCLAIMERS

An Inspiring Autobiography

Myesha T. Green

IISBN 978-1-9701-0918-4
Library of Congress Catalog Card Number: 0000-0000

Published March 2020

A NEW PRESS

TABLE OF CONTENTS

CONTENTS

DEDICATION

In loving memory of a blessing in my world

Blessing Hayes

To those who were not honored to meet you, I will share
the lenses through my eyes. This book is my vulnerability
and bravery to you. Every poetry event or presentation
I had on my agenda, I performed it to you. You can only
imagine how I feel right now without getting your approval
on my first published book. We had so many late nights,
walking and talking about our shared ups (as you ate your
cucumbers). We laughed, we cried, we hooped, we worked
out, we shot pool, we FaceTimed each other for approval
on what to wear, we got drunk, we attempted to dance at
parties (with our lack of rhythm), we watched movies, we
took pictures, we sang our hearts out in my car, we lived.
In our world we question so much, I am still questioning
not being able to hug you right now (you hate hugs). Your
smile and energy lifted my spirit every day. You used to
tell me that you looked up to me, but it was always the
other way around. All the tears that so many of us share for
you may never stop falling. I am hoping and praying soon
I can smile with those tears in memory of you. You showed
me bravery in you finding your happiness. I'll show you
bravery in finding mine. Thank you so much for always
listening. You will always be my blessing.

INTRODUCTION

I want you to read this as if we are talking face to face. It's beyond fair to say that life can be shitty at times. I am starting to think the only thing that matters is our growth process. Our lives are full of different roads; in a realistic world, it's impossible to stay on that one road your entire life. If you get lost, there are two options. Well, some would say three. You can ask for directions, try to figure it out by yourself or just remain where you are. At some point in life, you will face more than one of those options. I hope you're able to learn from those different roads that come your way.

Before I send you on a trip down my faded yellow brick road, I have a few disclaimers.

Disclaimer: I smile on the outside for the world to see, but internally I'm broken

Disclaimer: My childhood experiences are heavy weights on my ankles

Disclaimer: My short haircut doesn't make me a "he"

Disclaimer: When I love I love

Disclaimer: Everything really does start with self

DISCLAIMER 1

Do you ever have a moment where you are having a conversation with a stranger? They are doing most of the talking, but you are listening closely. That stranger is literally going through the exact same thing as you. Here are a few questions to consider; do you share your story with them? Do you share your story with anyone?

I smile on the outside for the world to see, but internally I'm broken. Let me put your feelings before mine because I want happiness in the world around me. I normally hear from people, "You are way too nice." On my good days, I get, "Do you ever stop smiling?"

To answer that question, "Yes, I do." Only when I am alone.

If I was the world looking at me, I would describe myself as a loving and caring person. "Positivity and productivity": it's a cycle that I want to help create one day. I'm learning that if we cared more about the world around us instead of only ourselves, we could achieve so much greatness in our society. The idea of being kind in a world that showcases so much evil would be a sight to see.

I'm doing it again. It's so hard to be vulnerable. Let me talk more about me.

When I look in the mirror, I see someone different looking back at me. Maybe it's a person that only I can see. That person trapped as my reflection is my internal. She wants to shout out to the world her pain, but it's only me looking at her. My world— well, our world— can't see what I see. Hey, world, this is me, trying to tell someone about that person who's trapped.

I hope you can bear with me in this process because, as we all know, images in the mirror can be unclear sometimes.

DISCLAIMER 2

My childhood experiences are heavy weights on my ankles! I always freeze up with words when it's really time to talk about me. It's scary, the idea of someone getting to really know you. If you could speak to me right now, I'd start asking questions to take the spotlight off me. Often, I find myself being heard when I speak instead of listened to.

Let's get back to these weights, tied down to my ankles. I was born into this world as a dope baby, weighing so little that you could hold me in the palm of one hand. It's a story that's way too common in the African American community. Both of my parents had an illness in the form of addiction. This was a world that I was not asked to be brought into.

I try so hard to erase the bad memories of my childhood. I remember the times I used to stand in line—no, not for the school bus or to purchase something at a store. It was the line coming out of the alley. "Myesha, hold this spot in line for me." Surrounded by nothing but strangers to me but friends to that dope addiction.

I must say it was one of the worst lines to stand in as a kid. At the beginning of the line was the powdered white stuff— that's what I called it before I knew what it was. I hated that powdered white stuff! It always made me cry. I hated what it did to my parents. Hell, I hated what it did to me.

Imagine that you're between the ages of five and ten, and you're just standing in that line. All the adults surrounding you are either nodding off with their eyes closed or itching. Do you see yourself yet? While you're at it, daydream with me. I used to stand in that line and imagine being at the park or doing my homework with both of my parents right beside me. That's what I called a good daydream. Blink your eyes twice, because it's over, let's get back to that line. After a while, that line became those lines. I do mean that in a plural sense. The most fascinating thing about those lines was that the weather didn't play a factor; hell, the time of day, whether I ate, what I had on, if I had to pee didn't play a factor either. Those lines were the most important thing.

For a while, I use to blame myself for the things I've experienced. When I was younger, they used to call me the biggest crybaby in the world. If anyone tried to separate me from my mom, I did this thing where I would wrap my full body around her legs. I would squeeze her legs so tight it was impossible for anyone to get me off her. It's fair to say I was a mama's girl. I think back sometimes asking myself what if I would have let go, or she wouldn't have caved in? Maybe I could have lived with one of my family members, and I would have been better off. Since I am on the topic of family members, it's time for me to put this question into the universe because I have been holding on to it for too long.

My family knew the addiction problems that my parents had, why didn't anyone take me away from that world?

I didn't understand as a kid why they kept chasing that stuff. I just felt like I didn't matter to them. Reflecting on those moments now, I know I didn't matter. The highness of that powdered white stuff clouded their ability to be parents, hell, to even create a life for themselves.

I remember when I was in elementary school. I am not sure which school exactly; I moved around too much. But anywho, one of my classmates was telling me about their weekend. She went to the circus and amusement park with her parents. While she was describing her experience, I tried to imagine being her. I am glad my imagination still existed when I was younger; I don't know where I'd be without it. Some of my other classmates shared things they did as well, but I kept quiet. All I did that weekend was play hide-and-seek from a dope-head who was geekin'. But it really wasn't a game. I didn't want to see him losing control of himself.

I have so many stories I could share about my life of watching the white powdered stuff take over my parents lives, but I don't think I'm ready. I do want to share this: I haven't forgiven my parents. Forgiveness can be so hard when you have so much anger inside of you. Most of the time, we use the word too lightly, knowing we really haven't forgiven someone when we say we have. We need to really give ourselves time to heal and forgive ourselves first.

My mom now has over seventeen years clean from using, and we have never had this conversation. I hope one day, I can be brave enough to tell her that I am working on forgiveness. I don't just want to forgive her, but I want to forgive myself for having hatred in my heart.

Unfortunately, my father is still consumed by the illness. He tries to pretend as if he's not, but I've seen it all my life. In my head, I just say, "Lie to me differently, sir." As much as I cry and want to help him, I can't. I couldn't do it when I was younger, and I still can't now. All I do is pray. When he calls me on the phone, I just want to break down, but I try to remain present. The only thing that helps me cheer up after his phone calls is talking to my older sister. We tell jokes to each other that only we would understand. "I was adopted. That's not my dad," or "You're older than me, he was your father first."

My father just recently lost his mother. It's hard for me to refer to her as my grandmother because I barely knew her. The few memories I have of her are not good. The first memory is more like something that was passed down. On my stomach, I have a burn mark that will never go away. My sister told me when I was an infant, my father's mother mistakenly burned me with a cigarette butt. My sister also has a huge mark on her leg. After looking at her scar and seeing mine, it's kind of hard to believe that it was only a mistake. The memory that I have of my own is when I was between the ages of six and eight. I am not too sure how I got to her house, but I spent the night. She woke me up early in the morning and told me to come downstairs for breakfast. When the food was done, I told her that I didn't really want a lot of food. The only two items that I remember being on my plate were scrambled eggs and cream of wheat. I am not much of a cooker now, maybe that's something I picked up from her because I didn't like her eggs at all. She made me sit there until I cleaned my whole plate. I remember crying and forcing myself to eat. I know this might sound nasty, but the only way I was able to get through those eggs was by putting ketchup on them. Surprisingly, still to this day, I put ketchup on my eggs. It sucks that those are my only memories of her.

I woke up extremely early on the day of the funeral. So many thoughts were running through my mind honestly. I was sad because this was the third funeral I had attended in less than 5 months. I had a forty-five-minute drive to make it to the funeral, so I had some time to collect my thoughts. When I first arrived at the funeral home, the first person I saw was my father. I've never seen him cry before! As he slowly stood when I approached him, I made sure to embarrass him with a hug like no other. I hugged him so closely, hoping that he could feel my heart crying out to his. After hugging him, he sat down. He was seated in the very front of the church (where the immediate family was seated). I was kind of relieved that all the seats were taken because I didn't feel like that was my place. I found a seat in the back.

Once the service started, my eyes were full of tears. I just stared at my father as if I was an angel watching over him. That entire service was an eye-opener for me. I met family members that I've never seen before! And most importantly, I was introduced to my grandmother through her obituary. The woman that was read to me sounded as if she had a beautiful soul. I smiled when it was mentioned that she loved sports because we had something in common. I really wish I could have had an opportunity to get to know the beauty in her, the way that the broken hearts surrounding me did.

Before they closed the coffin, it was time to say the final goodbyes. My father stood there with complete emptiness. My sister and I stood behind him with our hands on his back. I felt my strength leaving my body to go into his. I made a joke hoping it would make him smile. As I reached for some tissue, I said, "here's something to wipe the creatures falling from your nose." He looked at me and gave me a smile that said thank you without using words. I've seen my father at low points before but never like this. For a moment, I saw a man turn into a boy and then I saw a "see you later" turn into "goodbye."

Lately, I've been praying for my father a lot more. I believe that losing loved ones can sometimes push you over the edge. My father's addiction is making him sick. His time is limited if he doesn't take proper care of himself. It's sad to say, but I have my black suit hanging in my closet. I hate that I think this way, but maybe it's the way that I cope with things. When reality hits me in my face, I must continuously remind myself that I cannot help the people in my life or even a stranger if they do not want to help themselves.

Have you ever wanted to see life from a different view? I always say perception is the key to it all. I have a story that I believe I am ready to share. I was between the ages of sixteen and nineteen. I had just got off work, and it was so dark and rainy, and honestly, I was having a horrible day. If I remember correctly, I may have left my wallet home, and my phone was about to die. I had no way of getting home, so I started to walk. I had to walk about ten to fifteen miles to my home. As I walked, and the rain poured down on my face, my tears were unseen to the strangers passing me by. I saw a bridge when I looked up at the sky. I told myself that I wanted to sit down. So, I walked to the top of the bridge and sat on the edge of it. When I was sitting on that edge, the rain stopped, and the cars beneath me seemed as if they were racing to a destination.

After staring down, I eventually looked up at the sky, but all I saw was enormous lights flashing down at me. I was confused! I just knew the sun wasn't shining that bright at night. One of the cars passing by called the police. Everything was happening so fast! I was scared. I got to the hospital, I felt so alone even though my family was in the waiting area. There was this woman who came into my room. I was crying, but the rain wasn't present to wipe my tears away this time. She had a clipboard full of questions. Before she could even start to ask those questions, I started to explain my story of perspective. This experience, for me, was an example of being down but knowing how to look up. I wasn't admitted that night or any other night because I wasn't on that bridge to give up. I was on the bridge to figure out how to get up! That's my weird story of perception.

I'm trying to learn that these weights on my ankles are not negative things. Instead, they are metaphors for taking what life throws at you and using it to your advantage. Using my life as an example, I could have chosen to reciprocate my childhood environment. Instead, I've chosen to rise above those experiences. Here's a disclaimer within this disclaimer, throughout it all I know one thing: my damn ankles are going to be strong as hell. The bad seeds that grow alongside us do not define us. Smile at the world, even when it's not smiling at you. It should be our duty to help plant good seeds.

In everyone's story, things can be similar or different, but I know we can all learn from each other. I'm beginning to learn so much about my story that I want to use it to help others. There's a lot of areas of my childhood I didn't share on purpose. I must share this: my strength came from three things. One, not wanting to have the life my parents did. Two, having positive people in my circle who believed in me and three, playing sports.

I have a handful of beautiful people whose stories will always be a part of my story, and that's what I think is important. I want to be a part of someone else's story. Someone believed in me! I want to believe in others! Seeing the things in my culture that need to be changed means being a part of creating change. I want to try not just to exist but be present with my hand raised.

DISCLAIMER 3

My short haircut doesn't make me a "he." I am a lesbian! If that term is new to you, I'll try my best to explain what it means to me. I am mentally, physically, intellectually, spiritually and sexually attracted to the same sex, which is female. It sucks to say, but what makes me happy is put into a box for our society to categorize. Our society can do so much better. Honestly, why can't I just be a woman that loves women? Hell, why do I even have to call it anything?

Here's the story of when Myesha started doing that "dyking" thing! By the way, using the term" dyke" or "dyking out" can be offensive, if you're not a lesbian.

When I was younger, I was always considered a tomboy. That term annoys me. It was because I didn't get my nails done, play with doll babies, or wear dresses every day. Yup! Thanks again, society, for telling the world to label me into another category. I just thought I was a girl who liked sports, sweatpants, and sneakers; little did I know people saw me as a little dyke in the making. I swear everyone always said, "I knew you liked girls ever since you were younger." I guess they knew me before I knew myself. I don't want to spoil what's coming up in the next disclaimer, but I didn't always like women. I have been in relationships with the opposite sex.

I feared to tell my sexuality to my mom. I would hear her talk about lesbians or gay men, and she just seemed uneasy. One day she asked me, and it just came out. She told me she was going to pray for me because I was going to hell. I didn't know how to respond to that honestly. I wanted to cry and cuss her out all in one. I chose to call my big sister to try to calm down. I thought, "what gave her the right to judge my life?" Why did she think it was okay to look down on me when all my life, I could have been looking down on her?

I was so angry because I had accepted my mom as a drug addict. I used to get teased and picked on in school because of both of my parents, but I didn't care! I was a sad kid growing up but never ashamed. Are you ashamed of me, Mom, because I love women? Do I even really say sorry because it's my life, and your acceptance isn't needed, just wanted?

I know that when I find my wife, my mom doesn't want to be at my wedding. Doesn't that suck? I also know my father will probably still be using drugs because I don't think he cares for his wellbeing anymore, and I lost faith in him a long time ago. As much as I think about my future, it's unfortunate to see my wedding without my parents there to support me. I always ask myself what if I had a normal childhood growing up, but then I ask myself, what is a normal childhood?

When I enter a room, the first thing I want to just shout out so that it's clear is, "I am a female!" I guess my voice may not be soft enough, or my shirt isn't showing my boobs enough.

Society let me dress the way I want to dress! Let me wear my hair the way I want to wear my hair. Treat my sexuality as if it's an unknown name. When you do not know someone's name, you simply ask. Ask me, society!

Every time I am in a public space and I have to use the restroom, I normally try to hold it until I get home. Here's an example of why I try to do that. As I flushed the toilet and walk to the sink to wash my hands, an older woman walks in. She looks at me up and down and says, "Oh my, I am sorry." Funniest thing ever, she says that same line to me twice. After she leaves and re-reads the sign on the door, she realized the mistake she made. I simply smile and wish her a great evening as I hold the door when she re-enters. Trust me, my smile is by far a fake pleasant one because I am sick of your ignorance.

DISCLAIMER 4

W hen I love, I love. I know I am still way too young to say I found the love of my life. Silly me for thinking I did, three times already. Don't laugh at me too much when I go into my love life. I've been known to be a little bit dramatic. Here's the dramatic tale of my three lovers: one was a male, and two were female.

Let me paint a picture of this guy, so you can understand why I fell in love. We both played sports in high school. It was so cute. When I tell you, he was always there for me, he was literally always there for me. He would help me with my studies, sports, everything you could think of. It was almost unreal how real our relationship was. They would say we started to look alike because we literally spent every moment together. I was the thumb, and he was the index finger if that even makes sense. The bond we shared was just something I can still smile about today even though I no longer have a desire to be with a male.

I never really had a father figure in my life. I think that's why I cared for him so much. He treated me like I was everything in the world to him. I remember one Christmas, I was sad because I already knew I wasn't going to get much, again and all my friends would get everything that they wanted.

I knew that the holidays were supposed to be about family, but I was also a kid. This guy was my Santa Clause, standing at my door with a huge bag full of gifts just for me. He had to catch at least two buses in the snow and wait for hours to get to my house. There were so many tears that fell from my eyes, it was just unreal. Does it sound like a fairytale yet?

I loved that we both played sports. In my mind, when we played each other one on one, I'd think of us like the movie "Love and Basketball." I'm cheesy, yeah, I know. It's a must that I share this one story, though. I was walking to the store from my house, maybe a fifteen to twenty-minute walk. I was texting him the entire time. I remember he said something cute that made me smile from ear to ear. I was so into my phone, thinking about him that I never looked back or checked my surroundings. When I finally got to the store, I turned around and he was right behind me. He told me that he was walking behind me the entire time. I didn't even know that he was coming to see me that day. Now every time I go for a walk or even go to my car, I make sure to check my surroundings. You have to start seeing why I called him my everything, huh?

It's fair to say that some love stories look so much easier on TV. When we ended, we never talked about it honestly. Before we went away to college, something happened that we didn't plan for, something that was a blessing and a sin all in one. I always felt like he was there for me with everything, except this. The pain I had that day when my — well, our — blessing and sin no longer existed can never truly be explained in words. I used to just pray and cry for forgiveness so much during my freshman year in college. I was too ashamed to tell my family what I did because I didn't know what they would think of me. I was at a low space and didn't know how to get up from it. I think he lost me that day. I tried to make us work, even after this but it wasn't working out for me somehow. I used to visit his college, and I remember one of his friends saying, "I didn't know you had a girlfriend." I think that was the flashing red light for me. Everything was going so wrong in my love story that I thought it was going to last a lifetime.

Then, I met a girl in college who had the most annoying voice ever. She always raised her hand in class and would never shut up. I remember one day we were talking about birthdays; surprisingly, my birthday was the day after hers. She didn't believe me, so of course, I had to show her my ID to prove myself. It was a conversation that I needed to have because I was just having a horrible day.

You know when you see someone once, you start to see them more often. I started taking more classes with her. I think I liked being around her, but I never said that out loud. I used to go downstairs to her dorm room to use her printer. She would charge me one dollar to print things, which was funny. I am sure she knew I liked spending time with her because the library only charged you ten cents to print. Soon, we hung out all the time. It was weird, like when I woke up or if a day went by and I didn't see her or talk to her, I would feel like something was missing. Eventually, we became each other's secret crush. It was one of those things where no one said it, but we knew it.

They say when someone else has your attention, the person you left will want to come back. He started to call me more. We were no longer in a relationship, but I guess he was trying to fix things. I went home to Baltimore one weekend, and he asked if we could hang out. The sky was so calm, and the stars were so bright, it was such a beautiful night. He took me to the park where we had our softball and baseball games. We were sitting on the bleachers, just talking. He gave me a teddy bear; it was so cute. I used to love teddy bears. I made a mistake and dropped it. As he went down to pick it up, I turned around to look at a car that was passing by. When I turned back around, he was on one knee with the teddy bear in one hand and a ring in the other. All I could do was cry. If I am being honest with myself, my mind was thinking about all that we had been through and my birthday twin. The word "no" could not come out, but the word "yes" wouldn't either. The car ride home was filled with complete silence. After that day, I haven't seen him since. I know he is now married with a child. I am beyond happy for him, and I still have love in my heart.

The way we ended will never sit well with me. You are probably going to hear me say that two more times. I just really hate ending things on bad terms. I am a strong believer that the people you give your heart to should always still matter, even if you are just friends.

Dear Look-Alike,

I am always praying for you and wishing you nothing but the best. I want you to know that having you in my world was a blessing. I will forever keep your middle name imprinted on my shoulder.

Love,
Myesha Green

Let's get to this birthday twin of mine. I really like painting mental pictures. Well, at least I try to. I called her my queen! I would just love the way she would sing to me as I fell asleep on her chest. The way she dressed, her walk, her voice, her cooking, her smile, the way she danced; it just made me fall in love. The first time I saw her dancing, it was like no one else was in the room, and my eyes were stuck on her every move. I know I can't dance, but when I would join her, she had a way of making me look good. I hope that was a good mental picture for you.

At this point, we were no longer each other's secret crush; we were dating. Well, she was my girlfriend and didn't know it yet. I am thinking about the way I asked her to be my girlfriend. I was so proud of myself. I had written this poem for her and gathered all her friends into the lounge area in our dorm room. She said, "yes." I was so happy that day.

I know she was placed in my life to help me find myself. I would have never thought of being with a woman until I met her. We shared moments in time of being each other's first female lovers. We ran into so many bumps and one-way roads during our time shared. We were just so young and still trying to find ourselves completely. She always thought I was going to go back to him, and I always thought I was just a phase for her. I guess those things played a part in why we didn't work out. Those things were not the only factor that played a part. I feel like I just drank some truth syrup. In my journey of finding myself, I ventured off to other females. Now, I know I messed around with other women because she questioned the feelings I had for her. I don't want to make that an excuse, but it is my explanation. We ended because of our pride and lack of communication and trust. I follow my birthday twin on social media and smile when I see that she found her happiness. I hope that one day we could build a friendship because I will always be a friend to her.

Dear Birthday Twin,

You lit a flame for me years ago! That flame is like a trick candle in my eyes. The candle will never brighten the whole room, but it will definitely show you the beautiful paintings on the walls. Thank you for showing me growth.

Love,
Myesha Green

We finally reach Milkbaby. I only use this nickname because I know the love-hate relationship she had with it. How do those sayings go? Save the best for last, or third time's a charm. Honestly, I could write a whole book about us.

Please know that the stories shared about my lovers are only shared through my perspective. I always say there are three sides to every story: one being your perspective, two being the other person's, and three being what the universe experienced.

I remember the exact day I laid eyes on my Milkbaby. Hell, I remember her entire outfit. I had to close my mouth a little, I swear something could have flown in it. She had this look on her face that was so mean, but it made me smile. The first thing I did was tell all my friends that she was going to be my boo. I am pretty sure I told all her friends the same thing. It was so funny, every time our paths crossed, I would do cheesy things to get her attention, but then I would get nervous when she looked my way. She just made me want to blush, smile, and hide my whole face from her. Ugh, I had the biggest crush on her.

I found out from one of her friends that she did not like women. I tried to stop having such a huge crush, but then I thought maybe if she got to know me, I could get her to see more than just a woman. As time went by, we started to hang out, and I noticed that her mean mug face started to turn into a smile. Sidebar: you have such a beautiful smile, Milk baby.

When we started to hang out with each other alone, the level of nervousness was extremely higher.

I remember the first time Milkbaby told me she loved me. I think that's one day I will forever remember. She was this person that I adored and just loved to be around. The craziest thing about crushing on someone is that sometimes it can be somewhat of a spell. I mean like you are literally lost for them, or maybe you just want a happy ending. It was unfortunate that when she told me she loved me, I was still in love with my birthday twin. I was selfish. I wanted to adventure off because I wasn't completely happy, but I still knew that my birthday twin had my heart. Our relationship was built on top of hurt. I guess what I am trying to say is that I apologize to all the women that I hurt. Honestly, it wasn't planned, but I now admit to my wrongdoing.

I am a firm believer that the way you start something is the way it will end. In the case of Milkbaby and me, we went through so much pain. Sometimes I wish I could just fix us, but I know I can't. Four years have passed now without having Milkbaby as mine. I still have flashbacks wishing I could play in her hair while she falls asleep or just look into her eyes without her glasses being on. That's kind of an insider joke that she probably doesn't remember anymore.

We ended because we needed to grow apart, and we put each other through a lot. For a while and maybe still a little, I have been trying to get her to see me again. The things that I did to try to win her over haven't worked. This time around,

I can't win. I know it's going to hurt me when I see her really fall in love with someone else, but I want her to be happy. I must let her go. I am not sure when I will stop loving her, but I am glad that I was given the opportunity to.

Dear Milkbaby,

Let me continue to be brave and honest to myself here. I still love you. The more I tell myself that time or a replacement will make me stop loving you, the more I miss you. It's weird because I want you to have all the happiness in the world that you desire, even if I am not in the picture.

But on the other hand, I still want to bring you all that happiness in the world. I smile so hard thinking of the good moments we shared. The words that you said to me, "I am not interested," keeps replaying in my head. But it replays like a tape recorder that needs fixing. So, I've been trying to fix it, even though I know I am not a handywoman. I am slowly starting to learn, not only do I love you, but I am still in love with you. I am in love with what we use to be. There was a moment in time where we used to be each other's everything. I want to go back in time and freeze those moments because I miss you.

Love,
Myesha Green

Well, there's the tale of three people who truly had my heart. Once again, I keep doing this thing where I skip parts. I hope in my next series, I can be braver and talk about the dark side of me that came out when I hurt my lovers, as well as the people that I hurt that loved me. I just think love is like the cloud in the sky, so endless. When the sun shines, your heart is full, but when it rains, it rains and sometimes comes with lightning and thunder. Wishful thinking that the sky could just be full of rainbows.

My current relationship status is single. Honestly, I would like to keep it that way for a while. I am really trying to heal. Heal from the hurt that I've caused others and vice versa. I want to have hope for a love life but who knows how that will end up: after all, I am still young. I guess I will meet plenty more heartbreaks until it's time to find my soulmate. I am a hopeless romantic, wishing that I can wine and dine a wife soon. I guess a family of my own is such a desire because my parents didn't show me one. I am praying for patience. I hope my lovers know that the moments we shared were important, and I know I have grown from our experiences. I know that was a lot, but you have no idea how much I didn't say. I gave you a warning in the beginning that I could be a bit dramatic.

DISCLAIMER 5

Everything really does start with self. We cannot love someone in a healthy way if we do not love ourselves. I know I love myself, but I am a full glass of pain. We cannot grow as individuals if we don't learn from our experiences. Learn from them in a way that is going to bring you up instead of put you down. I know I have taken some things away from every experience in my twenty-seven years of living. We must try to let our open cuts in life heal. I have been putting a bandage on something that needs stitches. I have been putting make-up on a swollen eye that needs ice. This book is my journey to healing. Within my healing process, I needed to share some of my pain. My pain may be like someone else's or even yours. Self-healing is a process for self, but it doesn't mean you have to do it alone.

The way I look at self-healing is through growth. It's more common for us to forget about ourselves and worry more about others. Here are the things that I've experienced. If I'm being honest with myself here again, people say that I am an overly expressive person. I find myself caring so much about other people that I explain myself to them. I try to communicate differently with them, and I start to find myself changing to please someone else's needs. This wasn't healthy for my self-growth! I used to think that this part of me was a flaw. Now, I just think the only flaw was that I was trying to accommodate irrelevant factors. A lesson to self, accept all of you, even when others don't.

The world we live in is like a grocery store, filled with so many different brands of goods, services, and checkout lines. Those goods and lines are decisions in our lives. When we walk into the store, we either come with a list in mind or just visit every aisle. If you live alone, you are only purchasing things for yourself. On the other hand, if you live with others, the things you want from the store are not at the top of the list. Try looking at life as a trip to the store, and each time your items must be purchased first. When we start to feed ourselves first, we will come across more discounts and sales.

In my experience, in order to find myself, I had to look inside myself. Sometimes looking inside of yourself, you will find what you fear the most. I think we fear vulnerability so much that we really are not aware of the positive outcomes it could bring. Mental health is important to pay attention to. The support systems that you have in your corner won't know what you're going through unless you tell them. This book series is one of my support systems. I am hoping that I have encouraged you to find your healing. Your self-healing journey should start now. After reading the poems that follow, take a moment to reflect and review the reflection questions.

POEMS

My

My disclaimers are more than FYI's

My pain lies deeper than the tears falling from my eyes

My story is becoming my testimony

My tomorrows are the days I'm planning for

My life starts with me

We

We fear what we can't see

We believe in what's passed down or known

We love because we are human

We care because it's natural

We give because it's uplifting

We hurt because we hurt

We love because we need love

We fear vulnerability because of its layers under our skin

Break the fear, there is strength and growth in vulnerability

Smile

*I smile on the outside for the world to see, but internally I'm
broken*

*I smile in front of the camera, so the picture captures the fake
happiness in that moment*

I smile to avoid questions

I smile through it all, sooner or later that smile will fall

Imagine

My childhood experiences

Imagine wanting to walk tall but frightened that you're small

Imagine drowning in a body of water that's beneath your knees

Imagine being trapped in a room with the door wide open

Imagine driving with your foot stuck on the gas

Imagine squatting and taking a shit on the grass

Imagine the life you could have had

Ignorance

My short haircut doesn't make me a "he"

Although the word he is pulled out of she

YOUR IGNORANCE INSULTS

ME

Sometimes

Everything really does start with self

Sometimes it takes a lot to open up, but too little to get hurt

Sometimes we deserve better when we accept less

Sometimes we push ourselves to the back seat of our own cars

Sometimes

When & What

When I love, I love

What my eyes see as a desire, my heart is traumatized

When I give my all its conveniently the wrong time

When my wife says I do, it's not me, it's my heart marrying you

Father

My father's lookalike
I did some chopping, chopping not shopping just in case
you didn't hear me right
I guess this hair cut is what makes me my father's lookalike
Let me tell you what that really means because it comes off
your tongue with too much ease
LIAR, FUCKING LIAR
I learned the definition of that word because of him
COWARD. FUCKING COWARD
As my mother laid in the hospital bed, you left before the
doctor could finish saying what was being said
She would never walk again
You FUCKING COWARD
MISSING, you were FUCKING MISSING
Birthdays, holidays, graduations, games, award ceremonies
PRETENDER, FUCKING PRETENDER
That's my baby, my daughter, I was there through it all
My father's look alike
Naw I'm not my father's look alike
I'd be dammed if we looked alike

Dear Society

Dear Society, I am female
I do not walk around with my pants hanging off my ass nor
do see a beautiful woman and just think to smash
I do not answer to the word dyke or gay ass
So, excuse me as I roll my eyes and flip you off as you walk
past
I do not want to mistakenly be called he because in our
society my appearance isn't made for she
Or maybe my boobs aren't big enough for you to see
I do not want you to question me as I walk into the women's
restroom
Yes, I squat when I piss, miss
I do not want you to grab your purse as I walk past little do
you know I'd be the one helping you chase after their ass
I do not want you to assume that I have no class
You should ask my lady friends, I am a gentlewoman
Opening door, bringing you flowers until you don't like
them anymore
Kiss your forehead because I think you're sweet, I would kiss
your toes, but I don't like feet
I do not want you to judge me because of what's covering my
skin
I am woman, I am she, I am female society

Hidden

Hide me because I don't want to be seen

Hide me because it will help me remain

Hide me to avoid this pain

Alone Now

Have you ever felt your shadow disappear?

Leaving you alone without any sense of reflection from the sun

Have you ever stood within four walls in complete silence?

Leaving the room trapped with your inner thoughts

Having you ever fallen to your knees?

Leaving your head down because there is no hand reaching to help you get up

Have you ever watched the world around you move with a purpose?

Leaving you standing in the same spot, lacking purpose

Love

*Being young and in- love, the word love can
be defined differently*

Here's what it once meant to me

L- Lust

O- Overseeing

V- victory

E- emotions

This is how young love is defined to me

Life Lessons

We were taught to not talk to strangers

We were taught to respect our elders

We were taught to hold the door for someone leaving behind you

We were taught to raise our hands in class

We were taught to say thank you

We were taught to clean up after ourselves

We were taught how to cook

We were taught

But why don't we see what we all have learned

REFLECTIONS

Reflection Questions

D escription: Please note, there are no right or wrong answers. These are questions that I have created and answered for myself within my healing process. You are welcome to answer these questions alone or in a group. In my experience, it has been a best practice to do this exercise in a setting of comfort. In any exercise, what you put into it is what you will receive. I hope these questions can give you a sense of guidance to healing and finding self-love, as they've done me.

1. Do you look at yourself in the mirror?

If you do, ask yourself: who do you see looking back at you?

If you don't, you should give it a try for about five minutes (get uncomfortable with your beauty and or pain).

Takeaway: *Sometimes, we look for others to give us compliments. We are the first to see ourselves every morning, why not be the first to compliment ourselves. Maybe looking at ourselves reminds us of pain. We should try to regain our strength through our reflection, facing one mirror at a time.*

2.Have you truly forgiven who hurt you in your life? Can you forgive them?

If you have, have you told them?

If you haven't, do you know why? Can you live with yourself without forgiving them?

Takeaway: *Having hatred in your heart or holding a grudge isn't beneficial to you. Nor is it fair to the universe. I say that because every person that enters your life will experience your pain because you haven t dealt with it. Even if you can never forgive the situation, try to forgive the person because we all make mistakes.*

3.How often do you find yourself judging someone else's lifestyle?

Do you make fun of them? If so, why?

How does it feel when others do it to you?

Takeaway: *Throughout my experiences, I've learned that everyone goes through things differently. It's very easy to judge someone, but it's harder to imagine being in their shoes. We don't know what that person experienced in life to do the things they did. No one is perfect.*

4.Do you honestly believe that true love exists? Why or why not?

If yes, why?

If no, is it because you've been hurt too many times?

If no, is it because you've never seen it in real life?

Takeaway: *It's in our nature to love. I also believe it's in our nature to hurt, whether intentional or unintentional. We can't have high hopes for something we really don't believe in. I am a sucker for love, so yes is my answer to this question.*

5.Do you change yourself for other people? If so, why?

Takeaway: *Acceptance! Everyone wants to be a part of something. Most of the time, trying to fit in changes you. Be confident in yourself to know changing yourself completely for others' acceptance is not always worth it.*

6.Do you believe that you are in control of your life?

Takeaway: *Sometimes, we live our lives trying to live up to someone's expectations, or even for greed. It's important to be the driver of our own vehicle. The saying goes, you come into this world by yourself, and you will leave it the same way, with that in mind you should by far be in control of it.*

Conclusion: Self-love and mental health are components that are normally pushed to the back of the line. Treat yourself and the people in your life to the express cut line. The more open we are with ourselves and the people who care about us the most, the stronger we can be together. Thank you for reading about me.

ACKNOWLEDGMENTS

A special thank you to all my co-workers, friends, and loved ones who have helped me throughout the years. Please know I am forever grateful to have you in my life. Sending peace and love to everyone who may be experiencing something in life right now and may believe it's unbearable. The rain can be unpredictable at times, but I am a firm believer that you will not have to fight with your umbrella too much longer; the sun shall come out. Remain strong and stay positive.

I'm sure you picked out my outfit for me

It always seemed like my smile was bigger in every picture. You brought the best out of me.

We clean up well, the kid in black. Bless.

You hated taking pictures, but I loved smiling next to you. I will forever miss my best friend.

*Every cucumber in this world will
forever remind me of you.*

ABOUT THE AUTHOR

Myesha Green is 28 years old and is currently pursuing her master's degree in communication and public relation. She was born and raised in Baltimore, Maryland. She was a part of the first graduating class of Cristo Rey Jesuit High School.

Myesha has spent most of her life smiling. She believes that a person's smile will always have a story behind it. She aims to use her life story of hurt, her parents' drug addiction, the loss of her best friend, forgiveness, poor decision making, mental health, and self-love to motivate and encourage others to believe in themselves.

Myesha first found her passion for writing during her sophomore year in undergrad. Playing sports (basketball, volleyball, and softball), writing, and helping others brings out the best in Myesha's growing smile.